Weekly Reader Children's Book Club presents

MARLENE FANTA SHYER

Blood in the Snow

Illustrated by
Maggie Kaufman Smith

Houghton Mifflin Company Boston 1975

Library of Congress Cataloging in Publication Data

Shyer, Marlene Fanta.
Blood in the snow.

SUMMARY: A gun, a flute, and an injured silver fox
bring Max up against some difficult decisions regarding
their relative values.
[1. Wildlife conservation—Fiction] I. Smith,
Maggie Kaufman. II. Title.
PZ7.S562Bl [Fic] 75-14370
ISBN 0-395-21929-9

Weekly Reader Children's Book Club Edition

Dorothy De Falco,
especially in rain
and wind and snow.

1

On my way to school Tuesday morning I had some bad luck. I took a short cut through Clover Hills and met my enemy, Crow Hintz, who has been looking for any old excuse to break me into little bleeding pieces ever since I collected six more aluminum cans in the Keep Your Environment Clean Contest and won the bronze medal he wanted to win.

Crow jumped out from behind a tree and grabbed my lunchbox, which is plainly marked with my name, Max Murphy, in indelible ink over the picture of a couple of Swiss Alps. Crow said, "I believe this is my lunchbox."

"I believe you're out of your mind," I answered, and tried to grab it out of his hand. He swung it high over my head with his apelike arm and accused me of being a fat liar.

"Give it back," I said, and he let out a laugh that sounded like the brakes of the school bus — which I'd missed and which is why I was cutting through the woods and in this mess in the first place.

"What'll ya give me?" said Crow and he was smiling a very sinister smile, showing off all his teeth and examining the picture of the snow-capped Alps on the box. "Certainly this is mine," he said, and he snapped open the box.

"Hey!" I said. "What do you think you're doing?"

His eyebrows shot up. "Looky here," he said. "A juicy sandwich!" He began to unwrap my liverwurst and cheese and relish on a bun. "Mmmm," he said. "Smells delish." He wrapped it up again, very carefully, and I thought he was going to put it back in the box. Instead, he wound up his right hand and threw my liverwurst and cheese and relish through the air. It whizzed by my right ear like a line drive.

"And now let's see what we're going to drink," said Crow. He opened up my thermos of strawberry milk and poured the milk out onto the ground, where it left a pink spot on a little patch of snow still left from the last winter storm.

I couldn't do anything.

He is not that big, not that fat and not much taller than I am, but he is sort of vitamin-packed and different. Where I have skin and bones, he has girders and steel mesh. Where I like to listen to music, play jacks and write songs, he likes to choke, kick and break things up into smashy pieces.

When I saw him start to mash up my lunchbox, I tried to grab it out of his hands. He smashed it into the side of my head and told me to keep out of his uncle's campsites or go the way of the liverwurst bun. The Alps flew through the air and he smashed me again.

Clover Hills, which runs a half of a mile between the school and my house, is a short cut I've just got to use if I'm ever going to get to school at all. To get around the campsites, which are empty except in summer, could take forever and a half, but to run through all of Clover Hills takes seven minutes, fourteen seconds — if I don't run into Crow . . . or the traps his uncle, Mr. Janka,

3

puts out to snare little animals. (I have to be very careful to keep to the footpaths or risk getting a foot lopped off!)

Anyhow, as a final gesture, Crow took my lunchbox between his two big feet and crushed it with a boulder until it looked like a dinosaur had slept on it and the snowcaps peeled right off the Alps. "Turn it in to the aluminum recycling drive," he said, and then, still laughing, he took off.

*

"Outrageous!" Bernice said, when she saw me. Bernice is the crossing guard at school and — don't laugh — my best friend. She doesn't bug me about not playing ball (I don't throw too well); she lent me her tape recorder twice and it turns out she and I both like music and jigsaws.

"Was it Crow?" she asked right away. I had a bad cut, she said, under my chin and a blue-green bump was starting over my eyebrow. "There's a little first aid kit in the glove compartment of my car," she said. I cleaned up the blood with some tissues from a box on the back seat and a Wash-n-Dri in the first aid kit. I stuck on four Band-Aids and Bernice said I looked

4

Outrageous but all right. She told me it was better never to tell a lie but in this case to say I'd fallen down a flight of steps; otherwise I'd make Crow into a celebrity, since I hadn't even put a scratch on him.

At lunchtime, Bernice brought me a bologna and egg on white with mayonnaise, two Hostess cupcakes and a Coke.

I thanked her for all her efforts, although I wasn't a bit hungry. Some of the kids had actually believed the story about the stairs, but even if I could make the whole school believe that I could be this messed up from falling into anything less than an alligator pit, I knew I could never convince Dad.

2

No one was at home when I got there. When my sister Marjorie went to boarding school Mother went back to college and now spends a lot of time reading Medieval history. Dad works for the Vermont Marble Company and is never home until dinnertime.

I went directly to my room and began immediately to clean out my desk drawers because this seemed the best time ever to do it. Maybe Dad would be so pleased and surprised and distracted that he wouldn't notice a few Band-Aids pasted around my head. My Dad loves organization anyway. He likes order a lot, which dates back to his days in the United States Army. He likes things that line up: shoes, books, soldiers. And he can't figure out why when I throw a softball it travels through the air like a marshmallow instead of a rocket.

So I went through all my stuff and threw away all those things I can't stand to throw away because the minute the trash man comes I know I'll be needing them and then it's too late. When I'd gone through the collection of keys that don't fit any particular locks, my collection of stones that might contain semiprecious gems and the parts of an old chandelier that used to hang in the dining room before my mother remodeled the house, I heard someone downstairs in the kitchen. I called down.

"Mom?"

"Is that you, Max?"

"It's me."

"Are you hungry? Want a snack?"

"No thanks."

"You feeling all right?"

I told her I was just doing some work in my room and to call me when dinner was ready. I didn't want her to come up here yet; I'd caught a look at myself in the mirror over my dresser and

WOW — my face looked like I needed an ambulance. I kept my eye on the clock hoping that in an hour or so, when Dad came home, all the bruises would stop looking so blue-green-purple.

Next to Order, Dad likes Bravery best and I am not good at Bravery. If Bravery was a subject in school I guess I would get a D or D minus. I punch like Tinker Bell and I cannot pick up a spider with my bare fingers. It's a shame, because everybody needs Bravery more than social studies and English, which I am better at than everybody.

I needed Bravery now, because I heard my Dad come home and ask my mother for me. One glance in the mirror told me that bruises don't disappear between three and six o'clock — they get bruisier and bumpier, and no Band-Aids can cover up a whole face of lumps. When I heard Dad's footsteps on the stairs I rushed to the closet and, as a desperate measure, put on my big yellow rainhat that goes with my slicker. I sat on the edge of the bed and waited.

Sure enough, Dad looked into my room first thing and saw me sitting on the bed in my rainhat. For a minute he just stared. Then he said, "Is the ceiling leaking again, Max?" and I shook my head and my father said, "Shall I get you an

8

umbrella or do you think it will blow over soon?"

Then he took a step into my room. Instead of seeing my orderly desk, my tidy drawers and the wastebasket overflowing with things I really didn't want to throw out, he saw my face and his voice stopped in its tracks. For a minute there was a silence that hung there like cement. Then Dad said, "What happened to you, Max?"

What could I say? I said "Crow Hintz," and it was all I had to say. A storm started brewing in Dad's face. "Why did he hit you, Max?"

My dad doesn't understand that Crow needs no reasons. Crow loves blood and bruises, kicks and cuts. People like Crow keep Band-Aids in business. I shrugged. "I took a short cut through Clover Hills and he didn't like it," I said.

"Does Mr. Janka mind?" Dad wanted to know. Mr. Janka owns the campsites and most of Clover Hills. The town of Paragon, where we live, pays him to keep his eye on the rest.

"I don't think he minds."

Then came the question I knew would come.

"Did you hit Crow back?"

I didn't want to answer.

"Didn't you hit him at all?"

I looked at the floor.

"Look what he did to you! Not even one slug?"

If a gorilla grabbed your lunchbox, would you punch? You'd run! I should be congratulated for not running because Crow is sort of like a mini-gorilla and should be in a cage instead of going to my school. That's what I thought, but I didn't say it. Dad thinks Crow is a plain ordinary kid and therefore punchable.

Dad sat next to me on the edge of my bed and took off my hat.

"Good God," he said. "He really let you have it," he sighed and shook his head. "Listen Max — you've got to stand up to a bully. You can't let a kid like that get away with it. He'll do it again — and again, to someone like you. There'll be no end to it until you fight back. Remember how I showed you how to use your fists?"

Fists. If I got a D in Bravery I would definitely get an F in Fists. I tried to learn but my fists are not functional like some other people's. Dad can't understand that. It's like some kids not being able to sing on key. My fists are never on key.

Dad went on and on. He said a lot of things

11

about self-defense and showing your strength. Then he said some things about learning to be a man. He stared at me with the same expression he used when he put up the basketball ring over the garage and I threw the basketball ten times without getting it through the basket.

"Dinner!" my mother called from downstairs and I was so relieved I felt like racing down the stairs into the kitchen and eating everything in sight. But Dad had his hand on my shoulder and was holding tight onto my shirt.

"After dinner, Max, I'm going to take you up to the attic and give you something. Something very special I've been saving for you," he said.

There's a locked cabinet up there I've never been allowed near and whatever it was locked mysteriously behind its doors and had been waiting for me I don't know how long. "What is it, Dad?" I said. I was absolutely on fire with curiosity.

"You'll see after dinner, Max," Dad said, and he put his arm around me and we went off together to the kitchen.

3

We had fried chicken that night, I remember, and peach fritters and some other stuff I love, but I could hardly wait until dinner was over. I rushed through dessert and still had to wait while Dad sipped his coffee and Mom told him about her Middle Ages exam.

Finally, while Mom and I cleared the table, Dad went to find the key to the locked cabinet. It seemed like ten years before he found the key in the pocket of an old pair of overalls and we went up to the attic together.

I really love the attic and always discover some new old thing up there I haven't seen in ages, like pictures taken in the old days before I was born and Marjorie's first tooth saved in a little box and a bunch of hair in an envelope from my first haircut.

Tonight we went right to the cabinet in the back of the attic and Dad put the key in the lock. It seemed another ten years before he got the lock to unsnap. Finally, the door creaked open just like in the old monster movies and I felt a real chill as if we might find skeletons chained up there or bats that would fly out and bite us in the neck.

But, Dad shone his flashlight right into the inside of the cabinet and no bats flew, no skulls sneered; the flashlight shone right on a stack of ordinary little boxes on the left and a lot of dark nothingness on the right. No — not nothingness; something was gleaming back there and finally the flashlight caught it. A gun. A GUN!

Dad reached in and took it out for me to see — a big, real black and gold gun I'd never seen before in my whole life.

"It's a Browning Double Automatic," Dad said, as he held the flashlight up to it to show me the engraving on its dull gold side. "Your grandfather was quite a marksman. When I was younger than you are, he showed me how to shoot and Saturdays we'd go out and look for grouse or just practice shooting traps. I used to love that. Now, with so little open country left up here, with the builders coming in from every direction, there's hardly a place left to hunt. I haven't done it since you were a very little boy."

He put the gun into my hands. I just held it without really knowing how to hold it and sure enough, Dad said, "That's not how to hold it." All the time I was thinking that I didn't know if I really wanted to hold the gun at all. It felt very heavy and dangerous in my hands and the thought of shooting real shells at real targets made me a little uneasy.

Dad said, "I was saving this gun for your next birthday but I don't see any reason to wait any longer. It's yours, Max. Your grandfather wanted you to have it."

My grandfather died when I was four. All I remember about him is that he wore suspenders and laughed very loud laughs, but I did feel honored that he had left me this beautiful gun and wanted me to live up to it.

"We'll go down behind the garage, throw up some targets and practice," Dad said. He grabbed some boxes of shells from the left of the cabinet and still carrying the gun, I followed him downstairs and out the back door to the yard.

"It needs some cleaning and lubricating," Dad said, when we'd reached the garage. While I watched, he took apart the gun and explained its workings and its parts. "Twelve-gauge, it'll shoot anything," he said, as he showed me a shell, which didn't look terrifying until he explained it. Inside the plastic outside was powder, which ignites into a quick blaze and turns into gas; that's what propels the shot inside that flies out and hits the target. He put a shell into my hand; it didn't look that dangerous, just a red tube. It looked more like something you might plant in the ground if you wanted to grow flowers, but I darn well knew it wasn't harmless.

The sun was going down and I was a little relieved; it might already be a little too dark outside. We might have trouble seeing the tin can Dad intended to throw in front of the big poplar that borders the Bellwoods' property.

But he was ready to begin. He stood behind me and positioned the gun on my shoulder. "The left hand points," he said.

He stuck my right finger into the trigger. "Don't curl it around the trigger. Just rest it there."

The gun felt very heavy. "Don't let it sag," Dad said. "Now bring it up to your face."

The gun felt cold next to my cheek. It was cold out here anyway and getting dark. I was tempted to suggest we go in and let the whole lesson wait until tomorrow. Or next week, or next year. I was afraid I might miss the can, or drop the gun, or get shot in the head by mistake. Suppose the shell flew out the top by accident?

"Now look, Max," Dad was saying, "look down the barrel and take aim."

I did that. I took aim. I tried to remember all the don'ts. "Now, don't *pull* the trigger. *Snap* the trigger. Remember, *snap*, don't *pull*."

I didn't want to pull. I didn't really want to snap, either. But I did. Dad threw the can high in the air and my finger went *Snap* and there was a terrific noise: FRACK! and the gun hit me. It flew back into my shoulder and whammed me between the collar bone and neck. At the same time there was a faint orange flash, like those Chinese firecrackers that everybody says can blow off your fingers.

"OUCH," I said, when the gun hit me.

"That's all right, recoil," Dad said. "I should have warned you about that. Be prepared next time."

Next time? There was going to be more?

"Try it again," Dad said.

17

He threw up the target again. I took aim and snapped. FRACK. The gun hit me again.

"You're getting closer to your target," Dad said. He said I was doing very well.

The Bellwood kids — and there are six of them — had run out of their house when they heard the shots and were now running over to watch me shoot. By tomorrow it would be all over school that I couldn't hit the target, couldn't hold the gun properly and that my hands were plenty shaky on the trigger. I was ready to quit.

Dad hurled the target into the air again and again. I kept hitting branches, leaves, the air. FRACK, FRACK. I missed everything. I could see Dad's smile fading. The Bellwood kids didn't dare jazz me with my father there, but I could see it all written in their faces: Anybody could do better than Max.

Dad started throwing the can lower, and I took two giant steps closer. FRACK. Nothing. One of the Bellwood kids let out a half-laugh and slapped his palm over his mouth as if he couldn't help himself.

"You need inspiration, Max. Just wait here," Dad said, and he disappeared into the house.

Now the Bellwoods really let me have it. "You're missin' by a mile!" "You need glasses!"

"Want us to get you a cannon?" They went on and on until Dad came back.

"You'll do better if you think you're hitting the real thing," Dad said. "A larger target."

He held up an old stuffed dog I'd had practically since I was born. I used to call him Ruffy. I used to sleep with him during thunderstorms.

"Saw this in the attic when we were up there for the gun," Dad said. "Pretend it's a rodent. Pretend it's a rabbit!"

Ruffy! I didn't want to shoot at old Ruffy even if his tail was gone, even if one ear was hanging by a thread.

"It's too dark, Dad," I said, and I put down the gun.

"I brought a flashlight," Dad said, and he propped it on a rock off to the side, and shone the beam right into Ruffy's fuzzy old face. His little black-knob eyes gleamed right through the dusk as if they were sending signals.

"Dad, that's Ruffy," I said. One of the Bellwoods snickered, and I knew what they were thinking: Max is a big old baby.

"It'll have to do for now," Dad said, as he lifted the gun to my shoulder, stood behind me, and arranged my left fingers under the forearm, the right finger on the trigger.

I remembered all those years Ruffy sat on the windowsill in my room, propped up in the corner by the penny bank and looking at me the very way he was looking at me now. He was really good to have during thunderstorms when I was little; I wished for a terrible thunderstorm now, and rain that would come in rivers and wash us all out of this back yard.

"All right, Max. I'm going to throw him along the ground in the beam of the flashlight. Aim carefully. Got it? All right — *fire!*"

He'd hurled Ruffy a few feet off the ground and I snapped the trigger — FRACK! Ruffy flew apart in the beam of the flashlight, exploding into bits of fur in the air.

"You did it!" Dad said and threw his arm around my shoulder. "You *got* 'im!"

The Bellwoods applauded. "Yay! You got 'im!" they cried. To them, a hit was a hit. To me, it was the end of Ruffy. Dad switched off the flashlight and called over to me from the trunk of the poplar. "C'mon Max, help me pick up this mess!" but when I went over and leaned down to get the shreds of fur and foam rubber out of the grass, I couldn't see at all.

"What's the matter with you?" Dad said, when he saw me kneeling there, holding onto the tree.

The Bellwoods' dinner bell was sounding — their signal to go home. They all raced off, thank goodness, and didn't see what was going on here.

"Why, you're not crying are you, Max?" Dad said, with that edge in his voice that means he's through-and-through annoyed.

I shook my head, but it was true. I don't often, though I won't say I *never* cry. Once Mom closed a cupboard on my thumb by accident and I cried, but that was quite a while ago and I haven't cried since. So what was going on inside me now, anyway? I just had that awful bunched-up thing in my throat and my eyes were very filled up.

Dad shook his head. He didn't say much, just picked up the gun I'd left lying in the grass and started to walk back to the house. I had disappointed him again.

"It's too dark tonight. We'll clean up the mess out here tomorrow," he said over his shoulder and when I just stayed kneeling out there, wiping my eyes with the back of my sleeve, he turned and looked at me.

"Just what kind of a boy are you, Max?" he said.

4

As I predicted, the Bellwoods had it all over school about the gun and how I'd missed hitting the tin can two thousand times and how my father practically had to hold it over my shoulder and shoot it for me before I was able to hit a stuffed dog the size of a horse. It was the subject of the day.

At lunchtime Bernice let me sit in her car and eat my sandwich alone so I wouldn't have to listen to the kids. She'd heard about the gun and said guns were Outrageous.

I was eating my salami and egg and mustard

on white when someone tapped on the closed window of the car.

When I looked up there was Crow smiling in at me. I was glad I'd been smart enough to lock the doors front and back, because the person I wanted to see least, especially when I was eating, was Crow.

But Crow was smiling a friendly smile, which is so peculiar for Crow that for a minute I thought it was a case of mistaken identity and that he thought it was somebody else sitting in Bernice's car.

I turned my face away from the window and hoped he'd disappear, but he didn't. He tapped and tapped, and motioned for me to open the window. He wouldn't leave.

He wouldn't leave and he wouldn't stop tapping, so I finally did open the window a hair from the top to hear what Crow had to say, although I was pretty sure I wouldn't like it.

"Truce," he said. "Peace."

In view of my lunchbox yesterday and in view of what he'd done to my face, which still looked like a collage, there was only one thing to say.

"Buzz off," I said, and I rolled up the window.

But he wouldn't budge. He tapped and tapped and smiled and smiled. If ever there was

24

anybody in this school not to trust, it was Crow, but I couldn't get rid of him.

I finally rolled down the window an inch. "All right, peace. Now buzz off," I said.

"Wait!" cried Crow. He was smiling with every tooth in his mouth and so pleasant I knew he wanted me to do something I wanted no part of. "Shake on it!" he said.

"Fry an egg," I said, and started to roll up the window again, but he'd jammed a couple of his fingers between the glass and the roof and I couldn't squash his hand, although there was no doubt in my mind that he would have been only too happy to squash mine if the chance came up.

"Aren't you going to shake on it?" he called through the crack, making his voice good and loud so that some kids just coming out of the school yard had to run over to see what the commotion was. As soon as Crow saw he had an audience, he played it very big. "I want to be friends and he won't shake hands," he said. He managed to look very hurt, as if I'd been the one who had crushed *his* lunchbox and he was going to forgive *me* for it.

What could I do? I opened the car door and stepped out. Crow took my hand and pumped it for everyone to see. Then he threw his arm

25

around my shoulder, reached in his pocket and pulled out a package of Hostess cupcakes and insisted I had to have them. "Let's let bygones be bygones," he said, and although I love Hostess cupcakes, I had a feeling I didn't want to take any gifts from Crow.

"I'm not hungry," I said, and still, Crow wouldn't let me alone.

"How about a can of orange-raspberry soda? I got an extra," he said. He pointed to his lunchbox, which looked nice and new and was made in the shape of a United States mailbox. It hadn't been squashed flatter than a phonograph record.

"How about just giving me your lunchbox and your thermos and we'll call it square?" I suggested.

I thought he'd laugh at that, but he just stood there looking thoughtful. "Why don't we make a deal?" he said.

Making deals with Crow is like making deals with a vampire bat during a full moon. "Forget it," I said. I started to open the door to Bernice's car but Crow grabbed my hand.

"Okay, okay," he said. "The lunchbox is yours. The thermos too. Keep 'em both. No hard feelings." He shoved the lunchbox into my hands and now I was really uneasy — Crow is no Santa Claus and if he was giving me a present it might just contain a family of scorpions, a vial of poison gas or something that would blow up the whole neighborhood.

But when I opened the box, it seemed harmless enough: one thermos, one sack of potato chips and the can of soda — and sure enough — Crow's name was scratched on the lid.

"Okay, I'll take it," I said. Maybe he'd had a bout with his conscience, or maybe he was getting a new lunchbox and wanted to get rid of this one?

I started to get back into Bernice's car. I saw her heading this way; she was coming to the car to eat her lunch too and I thought we could just talk for a few minutes before the first bell.

"Wait a sec, Max," Crow said. "I have something in my locker I want to show you. Do you have a minute?"

"Well — " I said. I didn't want to go to Crow's locker for the same poison gas, scorpion and explosion reasons I didn't want his lunchbox.

"Five minutes, Max, c'mon," Crow said. "I want your opinion on something in my locker. Something very interesting."

What could it be? One of those phony boxes of perfume that turn out to be crazy wire snakes that leap out into the air when you open the box? A jar of rubber spiders he'd pretend to let go in the boys' room? You couldn't expect much more from Crow. Nothing in his locker could be good news.

Of course, now that he'd given me the lunchbox, it was very hard to turn him down.

"But I wanted to talk to Bernice awhile," I said, just as she arrived and was ready to climb into the car.

"Can't today, Max. Have to pick up my piccolo at the music store. I had it tuned up and Mr. Perlberg says it's ready," she said.

So what could I say?

"Okay, Crow. Five minutes. And it better not be anything that jumps, pops, squirts or blows up — I'm warning you!"

I was warning him? Very funny.

"Don't be dumb, Max. This is serious. I'm not kidding. You'll go for it!" He ran across the street to school, against the light, just as Bernice was starting her car. She shook her head and was she mad! "Crow is Outrageous!" she said.

5

He made me turn my back while he worked the numbers on his combination lock. I was still plenty uneasy. When I heard the lock click and the door creak open, I gritted my teeth.

"Okay, turn around, Max," Crow said, and when I turned around he was reaching deep inside the locker. "In here," he said, groping behind the books that were stacked on the top shelf. "Right back here — "

He pulled out a white envelope, bulging with something, and closed the door of the locker.

"Look at these, Max," he said, and handed me the envelope.

"What? — " I took the envelope and began to open it. Photographs. Dirty pictures, knowing Crow. I should have known —

But when I looked inside, took out the photos, they were not dirty at all. There were eight color pictures of Pearl, Crow's dog. Here was Pearl sleeping, Pearl carrying a newspaper, Pearl sitting up and begging. Pearl from the front, Pearl from the side, Pearl from the back.

He had crossed against a red light for this? Had he made me come up here, filled me with suspense and nervous tension for eight pictures of his spotty spaniel?

"You've got to be kidding," I said.

"You like the pictures?" Crow said. He had started to whisper for some reason or other, although not a soul was around. We, in fact, weren't supposed to be here either, but to Crow rules are meant to be broken.

"Yes, they're very nice pictures, but — "

"You really like them? Did you really examine them closely?"

I looked again. They looked like ordinary pictures one finds in ordinary albums.

"You know what I took these with?" Crow said.

"Yes, a camera," I said.

30

Crow threw me a look. "Listen," he said, "I took those with a special Revelation Instant 350, which I happened to get from my sister Alice when she got married."

"Very nice," I said.

"So?"

"So what?" I said.

"So, you know how valuable a Revelation Instant 350 is?"

"Well I guess it is valuable, though I wouldn't know exactly — "

"So," said Crow, and his eyes were gleaming as if they'd been waxed, "I'm willing to trade."

"Trade? For what?"

"I'm willing to give you the camera if you give me the gun."

So! That's what it was all about! Crow wanted Grandpa's gun! All this time the gun was what he was after.

"I can't, Crow. Out of the question," I said.

"Why can't you?"

"It was my Grandpa's gun. Anyhow, I've got a camera."

I didn't tell him that my camera was an old box camera that only took pictures with white streaks and I didn't tell him that I would have given him anything just to get the gun out of our house —

31

that it would be a great favor to me if God made the gun disappear, or break, or be stolen but that I couldn't give it away or trade it or sell it because I was 'countable to my father and the suspendered ghost of Grandpa.

"I *got* a camera," I said again and I began walking away.

"Wait a minute — " Crow said. "Just a minute!"

"I'm not interested — " I said, and hoped that anybody listening in the sky would forgive me for lying.

"Come home with me after school; I got an attic full of stuff you'd really dig," Crow said. "We could make a real deal . . ."

"Sorry," I said, and I was. I love attics and I love deals. I hate guns.

"Look," Crow said. He must have seen it in my face. "You come home with me after school and we'll just dig through the stuff up there; we don't have to make a definite trade. Maybe just a loan. Like I could give you something you could hold for me while I *borrowed* the gun."

"Like collateral?" I said.

"Yes. Clatteral. Whatever it is," Crow said.

"I don't think — "

"Oh, c'mon! You have nothing to lose!"

If I just took a detour to Crow's house after school, what would I lose, after all? With Mom at school and Dad at work, who would know? And I could just explore Crow's attic, looking for collateral — not that I would really consider a deal like that — and kill a couple of hours before dinner.

*

So after school Crow and I shortcutted together through the Clover Hills footpaths and arrived in Crow's kitchen just as Crow's mother was putting finishing touches on her newly waxed floor.

Crow's mother practically forced us to eat some doughnuts and drink a glass of milk before she'd let us go upstairs. She looked very surprised to see me, as if Crow had never brought a friend home from school before.

Finally, we raced upstairs and Crow pulled down the trap door to the attic, which was located mysteriously at the back of his father's closet and was dark and steep. This was great — much more fun than the regular staircase to the third floor we had at our house; each step made a sound like cats at night as we squeaked our way upstairs.

It was black as midnight until Crow pulled a string which snapped on a hanging bulb that shone a spook-light all over every dim thing.

I looked around and yes — it was amazing — there did seem to be treasures in every corner! Nothing like our old attic full of family souvenirs, a couple of old trunks and all my old sports jackets and galoshes. This attic was full of the greatest, coolest junk! My eyes fell on a moose head right off, with the hugest antlers and eyes that gleamed out of dark corners as if they could really see. There was an old sink with taps shaped like swans' heads, an old train set on a table, part of a motor, a lamp shaped like an umbrella, a life-size photograph poster of a man wearing boxing gloves and one of those old phonographs with the speaker and wind-up handle.

"Doesn't work, though," Crow said.

He started running around, showing me things — a set of bowling pins from when they put up the automatic pinsetters at the bowling alley, an ice-cream maker, a coin changer you wear on your belt.

"Anything appeal to you?" he kept saying.

Anything appeal to me? Everything appealed to me! I could spend two years up here and never see everything — ashtrays from the 1962

World's Fair and arctic ski shoes and a butterfly net —

He began going through a trunk in the back of the attic where, he said, *real* treasures might be found. "Stop me if you see anything you like," Crow said. He began to rummage through the trunk and every so often he'd find something that he thought might really get me to hand over the gun: a crystal ball on a stand, an old four-gallon hat, a pair of spurs — and on and on.

And then! My eye fell on something — something gleaming in the last dark corner of the open trunk — something flashing and winking at me, sending me signals through the dim murk back here in this corner, something I wanted like crazy!

The temptation immediately got to me. I felt hot and cold and in real danger of making a trade that would get me into red-hot water. I jumped up. "I gotta go home," I said to Crow, who looked at me as if I'd gone suddenly soft.

"Whattaya mean, you gotta go *home?*" he said, and he looked absolutely astounded, not to say furious. "Home? Now?" he said. "Are you nuts?"

"I have to go rake leaves," I said. It was the first white lie that popped into my head and I'm no better at White Lies than I am at Bravery. I always get them wrong and they come out sounding stupid, like I hadn't given them enough thought to make them interesting or real.

"Rake *leaves*?" said Crow. "In April?"

See what I mean?

"I gotta go. Thank you for the doughnuts," I said. I tried to race down the narrow, creaky steps and almost fell down into Crow's father's closet into his shoes and sneakers.

Crow was right behind me. "What about our clatteral?" he kept saying. "Weren't we going to make a deal?"

I ran downstairs and through the kitchen, where Crow's mother was sitting at the kitchen table having a cup of coffee.

"Leaving already?" she said, sounding very disappointed.

"I have to go home, water the grass," I said.

"Water the grass?" she said. "In April?"

6

Nobody was home when I got there. Mom was still in the library and Dad wouldn't be home for at least another hour. I went up to our attic and gave it a good going-over. Was there anything here that could possibly interest Crow? I couldn't give him the gun; perhaps he might like something else?

I *had* to have the flute I'd seen in that trunk in Crow's attic; Bernice could teach me how to play. Didn't she play the piccolo, which is just like the flute? I could pick it up in no time if she would just get me started.

Not that I wouldn't have preferred the trumpet, say, or the saxophone, but I'm not sure I have the wind it takes to get good sound out of an alto sax or French horn. A flute is something I knew I could play, an instrument that didn't need two people to lift it onto the school bus, an instrument I could hide under my bed, an instrument with such a neat sound I could get the greatest music to come out of it by itself, or play with an orchestra if I got good enough.

If. If I could find something, *anything* that might interest Crow instead of Grandpa's Browning Double Automatic.

I went again through the whole house; there was absolutely nothing to compare with Crow's collection. My mother doesn't believe in clutter and all I could find were old photograph albums, yearbooks and a wig stand.

But I did find an old jump rope of Marjorie's in her closet and I took it out to the driveway and began jumping with it to improve my wind. What if I could get a paper route after school, earn some money and buy another gun to trade for the flute?

Tomorrow I would skip the bus and begin running through Clover Hills to improve my lung power. If I got the flute, having lung power couldn't hurt.

This rope-jumping wasn't easy. I just wasn't used to it. My feet kept getting tangled with the rope and I kept looking down the street to make sure none of the Bellwoods were around to see me keep tripping.

"Twelve, thirteen, fourteen — " now I was getting it. Once you got the hang, it wasn't bad. Almost fun instead of work. Twenty minutes of this every night and I'd be sure to have pretty good stamina.

"Max!" Dad's car turned into the driveway and stopped dead ten feet in front of the garage door. I'd been so busy counting, I hadn't noticed him come home.

He leaped out of the car and slammed the door. "What are you *doing,* Max?" he said.

He looked funny, as if he'd caught me taking something out of his pockets. He said it again: "What are you *doing?*"

"I'm increasing my wind," I said, and he just stood there, looking at Marjorie's jump rope as if it were a snake.

"You're jumping rope," he said.

What had I done? Had I done something? "I was using Marjorie's rope — she won't mind," I said real fast. I hadn't hurt the rope, not in any way.

"I never jumped rope when I was a kid," Dad said.

"Well, I never tried it before either," I said, "but it's really not bad. It's fun!"

"Jump ropes are for girls," Dad said, and he wouldn't move, just looked at me.

I didn't know what to say. I just wondered who had made up the rules about jacks and jump ropes. Why were some things for boys and some for girls? Pink, for example, and blue.

"I guess it wasn't really that much fun," I said, and began winding the rope around my hand. "I'll put it back in Marjorie's closet," I said.

Dad nodded and got back into the car. Then he leaned out of the window as if he'd had a second thought.

"Come to think of it," he said, "fighters jump rope to get in condition," and he smiled and I smiled back. And then he said, "I came home early to pack because I have to be out of town for a couple of weeks. When I get back, Max, we'll go out together, do some shooting, right?"

I said Right, because I wanted to please Dad, but some little awful something inside me wanted to please me more.

Which was worse? Dad getting mad because I'd traded the gun for a flute or Dad taking me out shooting and getting mad later because I couldn't hit anything?

Right then and there, I flipped a coin in my head and I won. Dad would be gone for a couple of weeks; I'd trade the gun for the flute. And not for collateral. For keeps. I didn't want Crow taking back my flute in the middle of my flute lessons. I didn't want him to change his mind. By the time Dad got back I'd have the hang of it and once Dad heard me play, he'd understand why I had to do it. And Grandpa, I was sure, would be right up there somewhere humming along and applauding.

Except. There was just one thing I had to make Crow promise. Raise his hand to God and promise. I'd talk to him about it first thing tomorrow.

*

Dad had come out of the garage and put his arm around my shoulder. "If you want to improve your wind, Max," he said, "run. It's really the best way."

7

Which I did. To school next morning. I was practically the first one there. Of course, Bernice was already on the corner, wearing a yellow slicker over her blue uniform and a little plastic cover over her cap. It was snowing, April or not, and much colder than it had been the last few days.

"Bernice — I'm getting a flute!" I told her, and you should have seen how her whole face lit up, which is what makes Bernice such a good friend — when you've got good news she is happy for you and when you've got bad news, she's not.

"Outrageous!" she said. "Where'd you get it?"

I told her I had to give Crow Grandpa's gun and that Dad might be mad for a while but he would probably get over it sooner or later.

"Very good trade," she said, and she walked out into the road and held up both her hands to stop a truck so two first-graders could cross. When she came back, she said that I'd definitely got the better of the deal. "The only sound you can get out of a gun is 'bang'," Bernice said. "So who wants to play a gun?" and she laughed. "As for your grandpa, if he'd had the opportunity to trade his gun for a flute, he would have grabbed it!"

And she promised to give me lessons to get me started.

I ran into my classroom and waited for Crow to come. Of course he was the last kid to arrive.

Which meant I couldn't talk to him because our teacher, Mr. Grindheim, is very strict and keeps slamming a ruler hard on the edge of his desk to remind us how fierce he is. No one is allowed to say a word until recess.

But finally, after "The Pledge" and "America the Beautiful" and the attendance, I sent a note:

44

"Crow — The deal is on. Meet me in the Boys'
Room in 5 minutes."

I got permission to leave the classroom and
went to the Boys' Room and waited. A few minutes later Crow appeared.

I was relieved. I thought Mr. Grindheim
might not let two boys out of class at the same
time, especially if one of them was Crow, but he
is forgetful and probably didn't remember he'd
just let me leave.

"It's really on, huh?" Crow said. He was
pretty excited and kept hitting his fist into his
palm every three or four seconds.

"It's for forever, though. Forget the collateral
stuff," I said, and Crow looked very surprised.

"How come?"

"I just decided I'm a flute kid. You're a gun
kid. So why not make it for keeps?"

"Right!" Crow said, and he held out his hand
to shake on it.

"But — " I said, "you've got to make a promise. Cross your heart."

"What? What promise?" Crow said, and his
eyes got very small and suspicious looking.

"You can shoot traps with the gun. You can
shoot targets with it. But you can't shoot an

animal or a bird with it — or the deal is off!"

"Oh, for crying out tears!" Crow said. "What good is a gun if you can't go out in the woods and shoot a couple of rabbits?"

"The deal is off," I said. "Definitely no rabbits."

"Or squirrels?"

"No squirrels," I said.

"Squirrels are like rats," Crow said.

I thought that Crow was more like a rat than squirrels but decided to be polite. "Not to me," I said.

"Not even moles or chipmunks?" He was all protests and very annoyed at me.

"Definitely not!" I said. I once had a pet chipmunk named Harold and he was smarter than anybody. "Well," I said. "Is the deal off?"

Crow was mulling it over. "Blue jays? They just get in everybody's way and make a lot of noise. How about blue jays?"

I shook my head. "Take it or leave it," I said.

"Oh, all right. I don't have money for shells now anyhow," Crow said. He shook on it in a hurry because he was afraid I'd change my mind. Nobody wanted a gun as much as Crow did. At any price.

"This afternoon, after school, we'll meet in

Clover Hills in the East Meadow. You bring the flute, I'll bring the gun, okay?"

"Okay," Crow said.

"And it'll be for keeps," I said.

"For keeps," Crow said, and we shook hands.

I didn't know it then, but within a week, I'd be needing that gun very badly. Within a week, I'd know I made a really awful mistake.

8

I took the flute home and — believe it or not — slept with it under my pillow. I'd polished it with Mom's silver polish and got it to shine like a Christmas star and covered it with two Baggies. I wasn't taking any chances that she'd find it when I was asleep and begin asking a lot of questions.

I went to sleep thinking that while Dad was gone I'd work very hard practicing and by the time he got back I could be playing "Country Garden" or "Auld Lang Syne." He'd be so proud we'd borrow Bernice's tape recorder and tape me playing; he'd forget all about the gun.

When I got on the bus the next morning somebody noticed the flute sticking out of my jacket and pretty soon every kid on the bus wanted to see it. One of the Bellwood kids said he thought it might be real sterling silver, which was certainly a possibility, but seemed pretty unlikely.

"Do you suppose it's real silver, Bernice?" I asked when I showed it to her.

"Hard to tell, Max," she said, holding it up to the light. "It's pretty old and the marking seems to have worn away. I could have it checked out though. Mr. Perlberg could tell," she said.

"Another time," I said. I was anxious to get started. We'd met in my classroom as soon as I'd finished my peanut butter and marshmallow and banana on white in the lunchroom. Bernice was going to eat her yogurt while she got me started on the correct playing position and later she'd draw me a fingering chart so I could work at home without her.

"Leave the first finger of the left hand open," she was saying. "Never put your lips too close to the blow hole — "

Mr. Grindheim's head popped into the classroom. "What's going on?" he said, in his usual dragon voice, to me. Then he spotted Bernice, and I guess he was a little less fierce with her because she was wearing her full blue uniform, including the whistle around her neck. "I'm afraid I have to mark some papers in here," he said, very apologetic.

"We'll get out of your way right now, Mr. Grindheim," Bernice said. I gathered up my flute while Bernice gathered up her yogurt and we left.

We went next door to Miss Leafey's fifth grade classroom but the door was locked. Miss Dunleavey's fourth grade class was being swept out by Mr. Pullis, the janitor. Miss Almazar, the third grade teacher, was having a conference with somebody's mother in her classroom and the second grade classroom was being painted. The principal, Mr. Markey, was in the first grade classroom talking to the teacher, Miss Elking, but the kindergarten was empty, unlocked and quiet.

"Thank goodness!" Bernice said, opening the door, but instead of stepping inside, she stopped in the doorway. "Outrageous!" she said.

"What's the matter?" I said.

"Look at those little chairs!" she cried. "I feel like a fat Goldilocks. See what thirty years of mashed potatoes will do to your sitting equipment?"

I looked at Bernice and I looked at the kindergarten chairs. "We better not," I agreed. "Unless we sit on the tables — "

"Not unless they're made of cast iron," Bernice said, and we found ourselves back in the hall.

"How about your car?" I asked.

"Poor acoustics."

"What are acoustics?"

"Means the sound comes out inside out or flat or fuzzy at the edges. How about the boiler room?"

But it was so noisy in the boiler room, we couldn't stay. The storage room was too hot and the librarian said we couldn't make flute noises in her library.

So we sat outside on the school steps and that didn't work either. About a million kids gathered around to poke their nosy noses into my lesson. I could hardly think, let alone concentrate on tone production.

"Clover Hills!" I said, struck by inspiration in the midst of the commotion. "Let's go to Clover Hills!"

"Isn't it still a bit cold to play outdoors?" Bernice said.

"Not really," I said. "If we sit in the meadow, we'll be in the sun."

"Well — " Bernice looked at her watch. "All right, but we better hurry," she said. "We only have about half our lunch hour left."

It took us five minutes to walk to the Meadow Marsh, which is sort of in the center of Clover Hills and is surrounded by woods.

We found some neat sitting-type rocks near the edge of the meadow that had been really warmed by the sun and felt practically hot when you touched them.

"This is nice," Bernice said as she sat down on a rock, ate her yogurt, unpeeled a banana she'd brought with her and offered me a bite. "This is really very nice."

And we started the lesson.

That first day, Bernice showed me how to hold the flute, how to press the D# key for balance, how to hold my lips with the corners closed, how to avoid breathing after each note. I rushed home right after school to practice what she'd showed me before Mom got home.

The next day Bernice brought music for me,

showed me how to count and taught me the slur and the rest.

The third lesson was on Friday and she explained staccato notes and began teaching me "In the Gloaming." Over the weekend I went out to the meadow myself and practiced "In the Gloaming." Maybe not many kids would sit in a cold meadow for hours practicing a flute, but as I started to get the hang of it, as I started to get music coming out of the flute instead of just noisy squeaks, it seemed like I was celebrating instead of practicing and I couldn't wait for Monday to come, for my fourth lesson.

But it was very windy Monday and there was a light snow Tuesday. Luckily, Wednesday was perfect. Bernice and I went out to the meadow where she told me that low register tones are easier if you blow slowly and gently into the blow hole and announced that I was doing an Outrageously splendid job and to keep up the good work.

The fifth lesson was on Thursday and I played "Home Sweet Home." That was the day I saw the blood in the snow.

9

It was bright and red and fresh. The stain was really not one stain, but a few spots and streaks, almost like a Morse code message written in blood. There was very little snow left in Clover Hills, just a few sparse patches under a clump of trees on the outer fringes of the Marsh Meadow; if there hadn't been a sound I wouldn't have noticed it at all.

Bernice and I were finishing our lesson and I was stuffing the wrappers from my chicken and lettuce and bacon on pumpernickel into our trash bag when I guess I heard a sound, like a

54

mmrraarr, a little like a bass violin warming up before a concert.

"Did you say something, Bernice?" I said, and Bernice shook her head; she had heard it too.

It seemed to be coming from the right, beyond a little broken fence that bordered the meadow. We listened and heard it very faintly, but heard it again: *mmrraarr.*

I started to walk in the direction of the sound and Bernice called after me: "Be careful, Max!"

I slowed down, looked over the little fence, and that's when I saw the blood. There was a little trail of it, very short, and it ended behind a very large tree, which was really two trees that had sort of grown together. I took another step and listened and heard nothing; but I knew there was something behind that tree, something bloody or bleeding, and that whatever it was was waiting for me to discover it.

I had an awful chill and wished Bernice would hurry up and get down here — but she was standing where I'd left her and I had to go ahead alone. I had to climb the little fence myself and look behind that double-trunk tree.

I went very slowly. The first thing I saw was fur — a piece of silver fur — sticking out from behind the tree trunks.

When I looked closer, it wasn't silver at all, but had a silvery sheen where the sun hit it, almost like my flute when I first saw it in Crow's attic.

The fur was an animal's tail and it wasn't silver; it was night-black with white streaks, which made it look silver-shiny. It was speckled with fresh blood.

I took another step and looked behind the tree. Right away I wished I hadn't. What I saw made me sick.

"Bernice! Bernice!" I called. "Come here! Please hurry!"

Bernice, who doesn't run too well, came running.

"What is it?" I said, when she was behind me. "What *is* it?"

I could hear Bernice huffing and puffing. Her face was red from running and her eyes were very wide.

"A fox," she said. "A silver fox!"

"My gosh."

I'd never seen a fox this close before. And this one; why was he full of blood? There was so much of it everywhere . . .

"He's trapped, poor thing," Bernice said. "You see? His foot is caught in that horrible

jaw trap. It looks like he's finished, Max."

"What do you mean, finished?" I said to Bernice. I'd never have believed how much a fox looked like a friendly dog, a dog like my cousin Ed's really great mutt, a dog you could take for a walk or hold on your lap. He was looking right at me, not at Bernice but at me. His eyes were as dark as the marsh at night and he was terrified.

I could barely stand to look at the trap that had his leg in its teeth; the fur was worn off where the trap held his leg and the blood was sharp red there, seeping from the open wound.

"What do you mean, finished?" I said again, but Bernice had turned her head away.

"Come on, Max," she said, "we've got to get back to school. There's nothing we can do for the fox. Not a thing. Best to turn your back and walk away."

"You don't really mean you want to leave him trapped here like this?"

"Well, what else can we do, Max?" Bernice said. She kept her head turned away so she wouldn't have to look at the fox. "He's pitiful," she whispered.

"I'm going to let him out of the trap!" I said. I was indignant; did Bernice think I could go back to school and sit there and do math sets and book reports while the poor fox was lying here in awful pain, bleeding to death?

"But you can't, Max!"

I took a step forward, but Bernice caught my arm. "You can't!" she whispered.

"Why not?" The fox had his eyes on my eyes; he was begging me. It's funny how I seem to understand animals better than people sometimes.

"He'll bite you if you get too close to him."

"He won't bite me," I said. I was sure this fox wouldn't hurt me. He didn't have to speak to make me see he was pleading with me to help him.

I took a careful step forward. I knew I'd better move very slowly so as not to frighten him — but Bernice grabbed my arm. "Listen Max, don't be crazy! Don't do it! He'll bite. He doesn't know you're trying to help him. Foxes' teeth are like razors."

"This fox won't bite me," I said very quietly.

Bernice was standing next to me; the fox could see her every bit as well as he could see me, and yet, I felt again as if the fox were speaking only to me.

"He's a young one," Bernice said. She had

lowered her voice almost to a whisper, as if she sensed, too, that the fox understood us and knew what we were saying.

I took another step — did the fox move? I couldn't be sure.

"Max — be careful!" Bernice whispered.

Another step. I was held by the fox's eyes. Another step.

I was close enough to examine the trap. It was a steel horror, with two blades that squeezed the fox's leg in a vise, cutting into his paw with dull knife blades that had worn away the fur right down to the bleeding skin.

Attached to this was a long chain; the chain was fastened to a rock. It was impossible to cut the chain, impossible to move the rock, and even if I did somehow, the fox would still have the gnawing trap clamped to his leg.

I moved forward; the fox moved too. He was afraid and dragged his body a few inches, never taking his eyes off me.

"It's only me," I said, very quietly. I thought, if I spoke carefully, slowly, he'd understand. Everyone says foxes are very intelligent.

"I'm going to get you out of the trap," I said to him. "Don't be scared. I'm going to spring the trap."

"Max, you can't! Don't!" Bernice was whispering. "You're going to get hurt!"

"Bernice, pick up your piccolo. Play something," I said.

"What?"

"Please, Bernice!"

I had just remembered that Mr. Rodgers, our choir teacher, was always reciting a poem about music softening rocks and calming savage beasts. Music couldn't hurt the fox. And anyway, hearing the piccolo would certainly calm me down, not to speak of Bernice, who was really shaking-scared and pale as a piece of paper.

She did. She reached into her pocketbook, pulled out the piccolo in its case, and had it put together in five seconds. Good old Bernice — in spite of her trembly fingers, she let out some of the most beautiful notes you've ever heard. The way a piccolo plays in a meadow is the way I guess music would sound if it were coming down in a ribbon from the sky.

I couldn't tell if the fox was less afraid, but it certainly calmed me down; it was as if someone who knew more than I do had come and put a hand on my shoulder and said, "Go ahead, Max."

I took another step forward; now I was next to the fox, close enough to touch him. He had a re-

ally marvelous face, although there was the stain of red blood around his mouth. He'd tried to free his leg with his teeth, chewing away at his own leg, I found out later, and his eyes reminded me not so much of a dog's eyes as the eyes of a very old man. But the fox, Bernice said, wasn't very old, and I guess she was right about that; he had a young look despite a snow-white patch of fur under his chin that looked like a beard. The insides of his black and white ears still had a slightly pink cast and he had a dark gray snout and short, dark whiskers.

"I'm not going to hurt you," I whispered, and began bending over the fox to get a better look at the trap.

"Wait — " Bernice cried. She'd stopped playing and had taken off her coat. "Throw this over him, Max, and he won't be able to bite you!"

"I couldn't!" I said. If I threw a coat over the fox, I might hurt him more, or suffocate him. Even if I didn't he'd be frightened to death. I had to take the risk.

The trap was full of blood, too, and I'd never seen a trap like this before. How did it work? It looked sort of like a flattish circle with those two awful blades locked together tight around the fox's leg. I'd have to try to pry them apart.

When I touched the trap, I heard Bernice catch her breath. The fox made a sound deep in his throat and shuddered. "Play, Bernice, play," I said, and she began "Sweet and Low," which could calm anybody down.

I took the clamps in both my hands; the fox's snout trembled and I saw his teeth. "I'm trying to help you," I kept saying, and I just knew he understood.

He didn't bite me. His head was turned to watch and his teeth and jaws were practically touching me, but he didn't bite.

"I'll have you out of here in a minute, Fox," I said, as I pulled at the vise with all my strength.

It wouldn't budge.

Bernice, with perspiration running down her face, played, and I tugged at the blades until my own fingers were covered with the fox's blood. Still, the trap wouldn't budge.

Suddenly, Bernice stopped playing. "Let me try it," she said.

She put down the piccolo and went to find a stick; a moment later she was back with a thick and heavy one.

With her face red and streaming, she worked at the trap for what seemed like an hour. "I can't. It's rusted through," she said. She was panting, as if she'd run for miles, and the stick had begun to splinter.

Suddenly, her face turned white. The stick fell out of her hands. "Oh, good God," she said.

"What's wrong? What's the matter?" I said.

Bernice's voice dropped and her face looked awful. "Up in the sky. I think I just saw a vulture," she said.

10

We couldn't unspring the trap. If we left the fox here, he would bleed to death or die slowly of starvation. The vulture knew it and we knew it.

The fox's eyes never left my eyes. I'd failed him.

"You tried," Bernice said. She was shaking her head, pulling apart her piccolo, stuffing it back into her satchel. "And you were really brave. You did what you could."

"Not enough," I said. I stood there a minute catching my breath and letting my mind ricochet over the possibilities. "I'm going to Mr. Janka.

I'm going to ask Mr. Janka to spring the trap and set the fox free."

"Don't waste your time, Max. Mr. Janka is the toughest man in the state of Vermont. If he finds out you've been shortcutting through his land he's likely to put up an electrified barbed wire fence around the property. Remember when the Boy Scouts wanted to have a picnic out here last year? He said he'd shoot the first Boy Scout he saw with his pump gun? And his dog! You won't even get near his trailer; he has a dog trained to tear you to shreds if you set foot on his property!"

"I'm going over there anyway!" I said.

"Look Max, it's very late; we've got to get back to school. I'm going to have to run if I want to beat those afternoon buses. You'd better run with me —"

"Bernice, you go ahead. I'm not going to school yet. I can't."

Didn't Bernice see that I couldn't sit in Mr. Grindheim's class this afternoon with the fox bleeding to death, trusting me, and the vultures flying in circles over the trees?

Bernice shook her head. "Max, I guess you have to listen to your own music. Go ahead. Save the fox. Do what you have to do."

"I just have to, Bernice," I said, and I handed her my flute. "Take good care of it," I said and I started to run back through the meadow to Mr. Janka's campsite.

"Good luck!" I heard her call after me.

*

The dog was there, growling at me behind the fence. He was a shepherd mix with a black mouth and a growl deeper than a wolf's. He snarled a warning at me through his teeth the minute he saw me.

The Jankas live in a trailer that looks like a house with a porch and they've put up this wire fence all around it and stuck a mailbox outside it on the road. People say the Jankas don't like company, don't like neighbors, don't like kids.

The Jankas' dog certainly looked as if it was trained to keep Jankas' place private — little mean eyes, super-fierce jaws and teeth sharper than the blades of the fox trap.

I tried to talk to him through the fence: "Nice dog, good dog," but the only answer I got was HHHRGGHRG, a rumbly snarl that seemed to come right up from his stomach.

I wished Bernice were with me; if she could play the piccolo we'd get him calmed down in a hurry, but talking to him was useless.

"Hello!" I called over the dog's head. Maybe Mr. Janka would hear me and come call him off. "Hello!" The dog barked, jumping up on his hind legs. "HELLO!" The dog barked louder, sharper barks, as if he wanted to drown me out.

And then a curtain moved; someone inside had seen me.

"Hello! Anybody home?" I called again.

The door to the trailer opened, but not much. Someone was there, watching me.

"Hello!" I called again.

The door opened an inch more. Someone I couldn't see was in there, looking at me.

"What is it? What do you want?" A lady's thin voice called.

"Is Mr. Janka home?" I called at the top of my voice.

"He's not here!" the lady answered.

"Where is he?" I yelled. The dog was absolutely wild with jumping and barking.

The voice answered but I couldn't hear what it said.

"Where is he?" I repeated, and waited.

I couldn't see the lady behind the door at all. Why didn't she open the door properly and show herself? Why didn't she call off her dog and let me come up to the door and introduce myself?

"He's not here!" she said again and the door closed shut.

"No!" I felt as if she'd slammed the door right on my heart. "Wait—please!" I called, but my only answer was the dog's wild yow-yow.

What now? I had no Bernice, no piccolo and no more ideas. How could I get this dog to calm down and let me up to the trailer door? Suddenly I remembered something she'd said earlier, when I was trying to free the fox. Something I'd almost forgotten.

It was as if she'd come to whisper in my ear. Thanks, Bernice, I thought, and I started to run, worrying every bit of the way that it might not work, although it just had to. Had to.

11

It only took me ten minutes to run home. I'd remembered what Bernice had told me to do when I was trying to set the fox free. "Take my coat, throw it over him and he can't bite you," is what she'd said.

Wouldn't it work with Jankas' dog? I couldn't risk throwing any small jacket over him — he was too large and would shake it right off — but what about a blanket — a good heavy blanket like the blue wool one on my bed?

I ran in the back door and was halfway up the stairs to my room when my mother called me.

Oops. She was home, in the bedroom, probably studying.

"You're home early. Why are you home early?"

"I'm just picking up something."

"Picking up *what?*"

"My — " I couldn't think of a thing. My eyes raced around the room and fell on the flashlight Dad had used the night we'd had our backyard target practice. "My flashlight," I said.

"Your flashlight? At *noon?*"

"In case there's a — hmm — storm and it gets dark all of a sudden."

"Oh, Max." Luckily Mom was busy with her studying or she would have come right into my room to ask a pile of questions and caught me taking the blanket off my bed.

"Max — your father called. He's coming home earlier than expected. Probably tonight, so don't disappear. He'll probably want to take you out for more target practice."

"Okay." I couldn't think about tonight now. I couldn't think about Dad's face when he found out about my trading the gun for the flute. First, the fox.

I ripped off the bedspread and tore the blanket

72

off my bed, trying to be quiet, but I wasn't quiet enough.

"Max, what are you *doing?*" my mother called from her room again.

"Just fooling around," I said.

I carefully put the bedspread back on the bed. No one would notice the missing blanket if I remade the bed. I tugged at the corners and tried to be super-neat.

"Max!" There was my mother in the doorway, big as life.

"What *are* you doing?"

I stood there a minute, with my mouth going drier than shirt-cardboard and finally I said, "I took the blanket off my bed because it's too hot at night."

"Oh, Max," my mother said, shaking her head, "in *April?*"

*

Somehow I got the blanket out of the house. I ran all the way back to Mr. Janka's trailer with it rolled under my arm and my heart practically jumping out of my shirt. I hoped Bernice was right — if the blanket didn't work the dog looked mean enough to tear me into jigsaw pieces.

There he was to greet me again, throwing daggers with his eyes and warning me with snarly growls as I got nearer the fence.

I had to stand back a minute or two to calm myself down. As I said before, Bravery is my weakest subject and while it comes easy to a lot of people, I have to work very hard at it. I stood there taking deep breaths and thinking Be Brave. Finally, I unrolled the blanket, shook it out and held it in front of me like a bullfighter about to go into the ring. I stepped up to the fence and lifted it up over my head.

Of course, the dog went wild. He didn't like me and he didn't like the blanket. He was leaping and yow-yowing and dancing on his hind legs like crazy. His teeth were white, his gums black and his barking sounded like someone had put a microphone in front of his mouth.

One — two — three — ! With all my strength I heaved the blanket over the fence and it fell over the dog, burying him in a blue wool tent.

Yowl! He let out a muffled shriek, jumping around under there; I leaped over the fence and ran to the trailer like I was the number 6 shot we'd shot out of Grandpa's gun. I pounded on the door, panting and praying, because the dog was struggling wildly under the blanket and would be out any minute, ready to get even with me.

It seemed like ten years, but finally the door opened an inch. I saw an eye peering at me from inside as I said, "Please, call off your dog!" At last the door opened wide and there was the lady looking right at me.

She was holding a baby with one hand and a bottle of milk with the other; it looked like she was expecting another baby — probably very soon.

Right away she shouted at the dog, who had just shaken himself free and was already starting to head for me, "Down, Savage, down! Behave yourself!"

The dog shook himself and glared at me as if he was holding a real grudge, but he put his tail between his legs and did stop barking.

"He sure does scare the baby," the lady said to me. "I didn't want to open the door earlier — I hate to have the baby upset while he's eating. It was very clever of you to bring the blanket, but what a lot of trouble! You must have come for a very important reason."

"I really came to see Mr. Janka," I said. "And it *is* important."

The baby took the bottle and put it in his

mouth. "Well, I'm Mrs. Janka and my husband isn't here right now. Maybe I can help," the lady said.

"The fox is bleeding to death!" I said. I was so excited I forgot Mrs. Janka didn't know anything about the trap.

"The fox?" she said. "What fox?"

I told her about finding the fox and the blood and how the fox was going to die a slow and awful death if I didn't get to Mr. Janka in a hurry.

Mrs. Janka shook her head. "Mr. Janka had to go out of town," she said. "He just set the trap early this morning, though, so the fox hasn't been there very long. And it's a state law that a trapper has to check his traps every forty-eight hours, so he'll be back day after tomorrow at the latest — "

"Day after tomorrow! But the fox is going to bleed to death — " I cried.

Mrs. Janka looked at me very funny. "Well, I wish I could help the fox, but I suppose he shouldn't have walked into that set in the first place," she said, and smiled.

She smiled! I remembered the way the trap had been hidden, the sticks and chaff piled over the chain, the little hollow underneath where

76

the trap had been. Even the clever fox could never suspect that little pile of straw and sticks.

"I couldn't spring the trap," I said. "I tried, but I couldn't!"

Mrs. Janka shook her head. "Every fox is a pelt and pelts are valuable. Mr. Janka would be very angry if people went around springing his traps."

I couldn't think of that beautiful fox as a pelt. I didn't want to imagine him as a piece of fur hanging on a hook or being made into the sleeve of a coat. Mrs. Janka hadn't seen him and couldn't understand that although the fox couldn't say words, he could speak, and in his way, had spoken to me. Mrs. Janka didn't understand how valuable a fox's life could really be.

"And when Mr. Janka comes back, how will he get the fox out of the trap? Will he shoot him?" I had to swallow hard; I was afraid of what Mrs. Janka's answer would be.

"He can't shoot him," Mrs. Janka said. "The shot would put holes in the pelt. Ruin the fur."

"Well then, *how* — ?"

"He'll hit him with a billy club a few times. Don't worry, son, the fox won't feel a thing."

Won't feel a thing? Mr. Janka would club the

fox to death and the fox wouldn't feel a thing?

"If he sells the pelt, how much money will Mr. Janka get?" I asked. I could hardly speak at all.

Mrs. Janka smiled. "I don't know. It depends on the silkiness of the skin, the size and the primeness. I can't say." I stood there feeling just awful. She just didn't understand that foxes want to live too.

"I'll buy him. Tell Mr. Janka I'll buy him," I said, and I turned away so she wouldn't see my face. I wasn't going to let Mr. Janka wound the fox, starve him and then club him to death. I just couldn't.

I started to run back to school to tell Bernice. I'd get the money and buy him from Mr. Janka. I ran like the wind. I ran like a fox. I'd never run this fast before in my whole life, and still, it wasn't fast enough.

12

My idea was to present Mrs. Janka with so much money she would have to call Mr. Janka home to let the fox go or get someone else to spring the trap. My idea was to pile the money at the door of the trailer in heaps and mounds and piles and stacks so high she couldn't refuse.

Bernice had carried my flute and lunchbox to school for me; I found them both in the back seat of her car. Bernice was in the front seat; she'd been waiting for me. Everybody else was already in school.

I told her exactly what had happened, how I had to buy the fox to set him free. "Outrageous," she said. And then she said, "I salvaged a banana, an apple, a bunch of bologna and a half a liverwurst sandwich for the fox from the cafeteria"; she held up a paper bag of stuff.

And I hadn't even thought of feeding the poor fox!

"Bernice, do you have any money?" I asked.

Bernice went through her purse and found four dollars and twelve cents. "Wrong side of payday," she said, and told me she owed the money to Mr. Perlberg at the music store for some sheet music she'd ordered. "I promised to stop by with it this afternoon," she said, "but maybe, if I explain about the fox — "

I didn't know what pelts were worth, but I knew that Bernice's last four dollars and twelve cents were not going to make a big enough pile. Anyhow, why didn't I set up a collection right now, right here in school? If all the kids pooled their money, wouldn't I have a real mountain of cash?

"Kids don't have much money," Bernice said, shaking her head.

"Teachers!" I said. "I'll ask the teachers too! Why, all I need is a little bit from each one." I grapped my lunchbox and just about flew into school. I imagined I'd have the lunchbox filled

80

in no time — if Mr. Markey, the principal, would let me speak to everybody on the intercom for just about two minutes.

Which he wouldn't.

He sent me right to Mr. Grindheim.

And Mr. Grindheim said I'd need a note from my mother next time I dared to walk into the classroom this late; he sent me to my seat and told me to get busy on my reading workbook.

I asked Mr. Grindheim if I could please take up a collection first and I explained about the trap, the pain, the bleeding and the vulture. The class listened.

Mr. Grindheim said that foxes are predatory. I didn't know what that meant so he told me they kill chickens and geese.

But I said that most animals kill other animals for food. Anyway, this fox was no ordinary fox.

Mr. Grindheim said that people needed foxes for fur to keep warm.

But I said that people had sweaters and coats and long underwear and didn't need to use foxes.

Mr. Grindheim said that if we didn't kill foxes there would be too many running all over the place and we were doing them a big favor getting rid of them.

But I said that there must be a better way to get rid of extra foxes than torturing them to death.

So Mr. Grindheim just cracked his ruler on the desk and said that a fox was just an animal, anyway, and what was the big fuss about?

I didn't know what to say then because I didn't think it was anything to be ashamed of, being an animal. As I said, I've known some very nice animals and so far, no animal has ever smashed my lunchbox and knocked my face into weird shapes without even being provoked.

But when Mr. Grindheim gives an order, it would be like arguing with a stormwind to disobey; I sat in my seat and tried to do my reading assignment. Of course, the words just jumped around on the page and all I could see in front of me was a dying fox with terrible, pain-filled eyes.

Finally, what seemed like ten years later, the bell rang and school was over.

And then a spectacular, sensational, incredible thing happened!

13

Just when I'd given up all hope of collecting money to save the fox, Mr. Grindheim, instead of dismissing the class, walked down the aisle to my seat, took some bills out of his wallet, and stuffed them into my U.S. Mail lunchbox!

Was this really Grindheim the Grim?

He said, "I hope you can save the fox," just like that, and then he said, "Good luck, Max."

All of a sudden, all the kids in the class were going through their pockets and coming up with small change for the lunchbox.

Within five minutes, the news had spread beyond the classroom; it seemed like every kid in school was running in to put pennies and nickels and dimes in the box. Except Crow, of course.

Pretty soon Miss Alamazar, the third grade teacher, poked her head into the classroom to say she wanted to contribute a half a dollar to the Save the Fox Fund. She was followed by Miss Elking and Miss Dunleavey, who was also going to donate a little for Miss Leafey. Mr. Pullis, the janitor, stopped by to put a quarter in the box and Mr. Markey, the principal, said that he hoped the trappers could find new ways of catching animals without causing them so much pain and suffering; then he put a crumpled-up bill in!

By the time the classroom and the school had emptied out, the U.S. Mailbox was full to the brim — so full I could barely snap the lid shut.

I ran to the window and called to Bernice to wait for me — "Great news!" I called out, and she waved and said she'd wait on the corner.

Then I went back to my desk and lifted the mailbox; it felt wonderfully heavy — like a bar-bell or a boulder. I had to use both hands to lift it.

I carried it carefully out of the classroom and headed for the stairs. I really felt good for the first time since we'd found the fox; it seemed a sure thing that he'd be out of the trap within an hour. Surely Mrs. Janka couldn't refuse to call her husband even if he was out of town — if Mr. Janka couldn't hurry back, he'd send someone else to spring the trap.

And then I heard footsteps behind me. Someone was following me down the stairs!

I spun around and it was as if someone had punched me in the heart; Crow was right there behind me. He was smiling his Crow smile and in the dim stairwell his lips looked fishy-purple and mean.

"What are you doing with my lunchbox?" he said.

I tried to keep going. I tried not to stop. I even tried to run, but he already had me by the arm. His fingers felt like leather thongs strapped around my skin.

We were on the second floor landing. "Hand over the lunchbox. You know it's mine," he said.

"No! It's mine. You gave it to me!" I said. My heart was thumping so hard it felt like I had a bass drum in my chest. I wasn't going to let him have the money. Never. I wrapped myself around it and held it so tight the latch dug into my chest.

"Hand it over," Crow said in a voice so hard it sounded like it was coming right from Hell. "Just hand it over! I didn't give it to you. I *lent* it to you. Now I want it back."

"Fry an egg," I said, but my voice did not have any wham to it. I was plain scared.

"If you don't want me to mess you up again, Max, just give it to me. Otherwise — "

I held on. I held my breath and crushed the box right up against my jacket.

FLAM. He hit me so hard with the edge of his palm I thought he must have put a hole in my shoulder. BLAM. Again. I saw a little red streak when my eyes blinked. GLAM. More red streaks. PAIN.

I loosened my hold on the box and Crow grabbed it, wrenched it right out of my hands.

"NO!" I shouted. "NO!" I screamed.

But he had it, had grabbed it smack out of my arms.

"Listen, I need the money real bad!" he said. "Gotta have it, Max!"

Not a soul was around to hear; the school had emptied out.

This time I did try to hit back. I grabbed Crow's shirt collar and tried to punch him with a closed fist, the way Dad had showed me millions

86

of times. I forgot how awful I am at Bravery and I swung hard and really tried to land one of those perfect blows that sound like SOCK when the tough television guys do them.

But some kids are Fight Kids and some kids are Flute Kids and I'm no Fight Kid. Crow actually laughed when I hit him. He laughed a snarly laugh and pushed me up against the wall of the stairwell. I bumped my head on the fire extinguisher and fell down; Crow had the lunch-box full of money and he ran like a thief.

Which he is.

But by the time I could report him to Mr. Markey or Mr. Grindheim and by the time anybody found him and recovered the money, the fox would have died anyway.

I picked myself up and staggered out of school. For a few minutes my head hurt so awful I just had to sit on the front steps holding it in my hands.

Bernice came over to ask what was the great news I'd shouted about when I'd called to her from the window. I didn't even want to speak. I guess I'd never felt quite this rock-bottom awful before, ever.

Bernice put her hand on my forehead; I guess she thought I'd come down with some awful bug in the last ten minutes. "You look terrible, I'd better drive you right home, Max," she said, but I shook my head.

Finally, when I felt less dizzy, when I was able to open and close my eyes without seeing crazy zigzaggy lines, I asked her if she'd seen Crow.

Of course I knew Crow would have taken one of the back door exits so no one would see him, especially Bernice. She shook her head. "I can't believe it!" she said, when I told her what had happened. "I just can't believe he could do such an awful thing!"

She kept promising we'd recover the money. She'd tell Mr. Markey and he'd report Crow to the juvenile authorities. He'd be brought to juvenile court and justice would triumph and so on.

But I wasn't interested in triumph or justice or seeing Crow chained to the wall, because with my head spinning I remembered something Bernice had said when she'd first seen the fox. "He's finished, Max," she'd said. Now, with the money gone, it turned out to be true.

"You were right, Bernice, the fox is finished," I said, and the words sounded like little steel traps when I said them — jamming up in my throat. I imagined Mr. Janka raising his billy club, swinging it through the air, crushing the half-dead fox again and again . . .

I closed my eyes.

Then, like a little nudge, I had a new, last-ditch idea. One last possible way to save the fox.

"Can you do me one more favor, Bernice?" I asked. "Give it just one more try?"

14

What is it, Max?"

"My flute," I said. "You said it might be sterling silver. Remember?"

Bernice nodded. "But the *flute* — you don't really want to give up the flute?"

I would have given up anything at all rather than part with the flute — my desk with all its collections, my old camera, anything I'd ever bought or made or saved. I would have given up my bed and slept on the floor, if I could sell it. But the flute, if it was silver, was the only salable thing I had.

90

"Max," Bernice said, "you are a most unbe-
lievable person. Are you sure you want to give
up the flute? Is the fox really worth it to you?"

I thought of the flute and how it sounded in
the meadow and how great I felt when I was
playing it. Then I thought of Dad; I imagined
his face when he found out I'd traded away
Grandpa's gun and now would have nothing at
all to show for it.

And he'd be back tonight, or even earlier, and
what was I going to say to him with the gun and
the flute both gone? But I guess I kept thinking
what it would have been like if *I* were the fox,
locked in a trap, waiting to die.

I said, "The fox comes first."

"Okay," Bernice said. She had become very
businesslike, the way she gets when there is a
lot of traffic in front of the school. "I'll go speak
to Mr. Perlberg, but don't get your hopes up too
high. Silver flutes do not grow in attics. It was
probably secondhand even when Crow's sister
played it; it looks pretty old and beat-up. It's
probably only nickel, so don't count on it, Max."

In my heart I felt it *had* to be silver. I couldn't
let myself think anything else. The pure way
the notes sounded when I was getting the hang
of "Long, Long Ago" — wasn't that proof enough

it couldn't be *nickel?* The clear way the melody hung in the air — could it have been anything less than sterling?

"I'll stay with the fox. I'll wait for you there, Bernice," I said.

I was so sure.

I felt it all in a bunch inside me — a fresh batch of hope. I imagined how fantastically free the fox would feel when the trap was sprung, how in time his leg would heal, the pain would go away and he would cut loose and live peacefully in the forest again.

Would he remember me for the rest of his life?

Even if I got to be as old as Grandpa, I would never forget him.

The fox was right where I'd left him, but I could barely stand to look at his leg. He had chewed away at his own flesh and fur, trying to free himself — down to the white leg bone. Blood was everywhere.

I felt sick and had to look away.

Aim for an A in Bravery, I reminded myself, and I reached for the sack of food Bernice had salvaged and took out the liverwurst sandwich. The fox's eyes were dull and black as macadam, but they were looking at me and watching me.

Again I though they were speaking, pleading in that special fox way.

"I brought you something to eat," I said. I spoke in a very quiet voice so as not to frighten him. I moved ahead one little step at a time and tried not to look at all the blood. The patch of snow had just about melted away but the ground, the chaff and a nearby mound of moss were also covered with bright red smears. The fox's mouth was ringed in red streaks.

I could even smell it.

I moved ahead, put the liverwurst sandwich practically under the fox's mouth. "It's from Bernice," I whispered. It was something to say. I thought he wanted me to talk to him; it was a feeling I had.

The fox looked at me. His eyes looked very sick. He made no move to eat.

Of course not. Foxes don't eat sandwiches. The banana, maybe? I would try the banana. He must be hungry!

I peeled it, and broke it into chunks. I carried the pieces carefully over to the fox, put them beside his nose so he could smell them. But he wouldn't eat. Was he afraid, or too weak?

Or, was he *thirsty?*

Thirsty! I hadn't really thought of bringing water to the fox. He was probably very thirsty!

Once there had been a real marsh at Marsh Meadow but now there was not a pond, or brook, or creek anywhere in Clover Hills!

*

How would I bring water to the fox and why hadn't I thought of bringing water in a cup from the school water fountain?

Maybe if I walked a bit further into the woods I'd find some snow patches left. Between the trees, where there is never any sun, snow seems to stay on the ground for a very long time.

If I held my hands tight together, cupped them to make a little bowl, lined them with leaves and carried the snow to the fox, it might melt enough to give him a drink. The leaves would keep the melted snow from seeping out and he could sip, if he wanted to.

"I'll be right back," I said to the fox and grabbed some leaves from the lowest branches of a nearby tree.

I took a few steps into the woods to look around.

Nothing. I would have to go deeper into the forest where the trees were denser. I wasn't used to walking in this thick part of Clover Hills, but I was pretty sure if I kept to the footpaths I'd be safe.

Although, the deeper into the woods I went, the darker it got. On all sides of me were really immense trees. It was like walking into night; at every step the light grew dimmer. I didn't really like the mystery feeling of murky secrets all around me. Things hiding everywhere. I heard rustling sounds and fluttering sounds and swishing sounds. It seemed like things were moving on every side and yet I couldn't see any life at all.

Every couple of steps I stopped dead-still to listen and look. Not only could I not find snow, I kept thinking there were creatures ready to pop out from behind trees and grab me by the throat — the same watch-out feeling I get in the fun house at the amusement park.

For a few minutes I got really silly-nervous, remembering all the bedtime-type stories I'd heard when I was a little kid, expecting trolls and witches and whatnots to suddenly fly out and grab me. Ridiculous! And then finally I saw it — a neat big patch of snow still crisp-white as the inside of Mom's freezer.

There! I really hadn't gone too far at all; it

only seemed endless — a couple of turns of the footpath and here was plenty of snow just waiting to be scooped up.

I pulled the leaves I'd brought out of my pockets and began to line my palms with them, when all of a sudden — FRACK — I got the absolute scare of my life.

15

FRACK! RRRACK!

I must have jumped right off the ground I got such a start — the gunfire was loud enough to put holes in my eardrums when it came unexpected like that in the middle of a big hunk of silence.

FFRRACK! Again. Gunfire. It sounded as if it were coming from right next to my head; it was that close.

FRACK, FRACK, FRACK. Should I run? If I ran, would I get shot? Who would dare to be shooting in Janka's woods, anyway?

Unless! Perhaps Mr. Janka had come back early, like Dad? Perhaps Mrs. Janka had thought things over and called Mr. Janka to come home after all?

It might be Mr. Janka and he might be coming to save the fox!

"HELLO!" I called. No answer. "HELLO!" Couldn't he hear me?

"HELLOO!" I called at the top of my voice. "HELLOOO! HELLOOO!"

The gunfire stopped and now there was nothing but dead-sea silence around me.

"I'M HERE, WHERE ARE YOU?" I called. Silence.

"HERE! HERE! DON'T SHOOT!" I called. I was scared through and through — someone was here in the woods with me and it was someone unfriendly; I could feel it. If he wasn't unfriendly, why didn't he answer when I called? And come to think of it, if it was Mr. Janka, why wasn't he checking his traps instead of shooting his gun?

I stood there with my shoes practically growing into the ground under my feet. I'd heard a noise; someone was coming. I felt as if the ground were rocking under my feet I was so scared.

"HEY, DUMMY!"

I spun around at the sound of the too-familiar voice.

"Crow!"

"Look at this!" Crow said. He was holding Grandpa's gun in his right hand. In his other hand was the rabbit he'd shot dead with it. He had it by the ears and he was holding it high, as if he was very proud of what he'd done to it.

I had a very up and down feeling in the pit of my stomach as if I might throw up. I had to swallow a couple of times, and close my eyes and try not to see that mangled rabbit with his fur torn apart by shot.

"But you *promised*," was all I could finally say. "You swore you wouldn't kill anything — never with my gun. You *promised!*"

"I had my fingers crossed when I made that promise, Max. Besides, I didn't have money for shells then. But today, when you took up a collection, why, it was just my luck.

"I ran into Wally's Sporting Goods on the way home from school, plunked down the money and bought the shot. For a minute there they had me worried, too. Weren't going to sell shells to a kid 'till I told 'em it was for my uncle. After that — no trouble."

All the while he was talking, Crow was dangling that rabbit as if it were a trophy he'd won for running a fast mile or something else you could hold your chin up high and be proud of.

And all along I was feeling green and ready to throw up. I wished for sudden strength, for muscles like rocks, for arms that I could wrap around Crow's neck until I had him screaming on his knees in the pine needles — but this was no fairy tale with trolls and witches; I was still Max and Crow was still Crow and Crow had the gun and the shells and a fierce, hard, heart. All I had was an aptitude for Social Studies and Music Education and not a bit of aptitude for important things like breaking Crow in half.

"Give me the gun!" I said, but I might have been talking to myself.

He laughed, sounding like something that belonged in a zoo with bars around it. "For keeps you said, remember?" and he threw back his head and laughed again. Then he turned around, put the gun over his shoulder, and stomped back into the woods, clumping through the trees with his big mountain boots, while I had to hang onto the trunk of an evergreen until I got over my big wave of Crow-sickness.

*

Finally, when Crow was gone, I got what I came for. I fitted my palm with leaves, scooped up the snow and headed back to the meadow on the footpath. "I'm coming, Fox," I said and I ran back to the double-trunk tree as if I were doing the four-minute mile so the snow wouldn't melt and run through my fingers before I got to him.

"I'm coming, I'm coming," I kept calling, sure that he would hear and understand.

I reached him, out of breath and happy to be out of the forest again, but one look at the fox and my heart went colder than the snow in my hands. I dropped to my knees.

"Oh, no. He's dead," I said.

16

I don't know how long I knelt there just staring at the fox and feeling as if I'd lost a whole war all by myself.

I got to thinking about how nobody cared except me and Bernice, how other people were at home doing everyday things like eating and sleeping while the fox lay here dead in his trap. While I sat staring at him, his eyes shut tight, his body still, I tried to understand how people like Mr. Janka could be napping or smoking or telling jokes in other places while their traps were killing little animals inch by inch, squeezing the life right out of them.

I tried to understand how Crow could think it was fun to catch a bunny in the stomach with a shell and watch it die right in front of him in the meadow.

"I don't understand," I said out loud to myself and — oh — I had to look again — had the fox moved?

Did his chin tremble or was it my imagination?

It was darker now, and harder to tell. I moved closer — and still closer. Yes! I saw his stomach rise and fall just a little — he was — yes — alive!

"Oh, Fox," I said, and his eyes opened, "It's Max. I'm here."

He was alive, and his chin, his beautiful, pointed chin moved again, tried to lift itself to greet me; he knew it was me, I was sure.

"I brought you a drink, Fox," I said, and as I approached, his eyes opened wider and he tried to lift his head, but couldn't.

"Try to drink, Fox," I said, and I tried to fit my hands under his snout, holding the melting water-snow where he could reach it.

But he wouldn't drink.

"Aren't you thirsty, Fox?" I said.

His eyes didn't look like the eyes of a young fox any more; the life and gleam had gone out of them.

The fox was dying.

"Aren't you going to take a little, Fox?"

Why wouldn't he drink? He had to be thirsty, lying here God knows how long. Just a drop —

"A sip?"

But he moved his head away, turned his chin, telling me something.

And then — oh, no — not one vulture but two — suddenly came circling overhead like horrid shadows from a bad dream, circling, dipping, without a sound or warning. Now three, with wings as still as cardboard painted dead-black, silently swooping and soaring. Now four. Waiting.

"Get out! Go! Fly away!" I screamed up at them, and as if the sky wanted to answer me, it started to rain.

The rain came, a little at first, and then it began to pound down as if even the storm clouds were furious at me for meddling with Mr. Janka's catch. The rain poured down on the poor fox and I took off my jacket and covered him with it. I hardly felt the water pouring down my own back; I just sat there listening to the spattering drops and the shots Crow was firing with Grandpa's gun, and waiting for Bernice.

All the while, the fox's eyes were open, looking at me.

Hurry, Bernice, time is running out.

Hurry, Bernice.

Please, hurry.

At last, just before it turned really dark, I saw a yellow slicker moving towards me through the trees.

Bernice!

Then, just as she was close enough to see me waving at her, a terrible, riveting shriek came tearing through the woods.

YEEEEAAOOOEEEE —

Terrifying. It was a scream that sounded loud enough to tear a hole in the sky.

What was it?

YEEEAAEEEEEOOOOW!

What sort of creature could let out such a pitiful cry?

17

Bernice stood frozen on the footpath as we heard it again.

"YEEEEAAOOOEEE —"

It sounded like murder.

"HELP! HELLLLP!"

It sounded like Crow.

Crow!

I rushed over to Bernice. "Something's happened to Crow!" I said.

"HELP! HELP ME!" His voice ricocheted through the trees; there seemed to be a dozen

Crow voices screaming for help through the forest. All the voices sounded strangled and terrified.

I followed the sound, running off the footpath in the direction of the East Meadow, where the trees thin out and there's a grassy area bordered by rocks and shrubs. In summer clover and buttercups sprout all over the place giving the grass a sort of yellow carpet, but now the field was soggy with rain and gray and squishy-awful to walk through. Still, I ran so fast, I hardly noticed the mud mushing up around my shoes.

Bernice huffed and puffed behind me; the rain was fierce.

"Crow! Where are you?" I yelled.

"HELP! HERE!" The voice came from behind the huckleberry shrubs straight ahead at the edge of the field.

"We're coming! We're coming!" I called, beginning to huff and puff a little myself. I tried to imagine what could have happened to Crow; it was hard to picture a tough kid like Crow needing my help, screaming like my sister Marjorie screams when she sees a snake.

The huckleberry shrubs were wet and scratchy when I pushed my way through them. They tangled here and there, pasted themselves across my face, caught in my shirt and dripped even more cold rain down the back of my neck.

Behind the shrubs, in the clearing, there he was.

Crow was half-sitting, half-lying against an old stump, the steel jaws of another of Mr. Janka's traps gripping his mountain boot around the ankle.

"Whoosh!" I cried. I nearly fell backwards, I was so surprised.

"Don't laugh, it's not funny!" Crow said, very snippy.

"I wasn't laughing," I said.

"It hurts," Crow said.

"But not much. It's got your boot," I pointed out. "It's not clamping your skin. There's not even a drop of blood." I said.

"It hurts like the devil," Crow said. He started to cry, actually cry. He was wiping his eyes with the back of his hand and he didn't want me to see how his eyes were filling right up again.

Crow crying? I didn't think Crow had any tears stored up in that tough, steel-girdered head of his.

"Come on," he said, "get me out of here, will-ya?"

I just stood there a minute, looking at him in the trap, letting it all sink in.

"Please!" It was Crow's voice, but all the fists had gone right out of it. You could almost feel sorry for him, chained up like that and scared out of his wits, with his voice coming out weaker than a cup of tea. You could almost feel sorry for him until you saw the gun lying there next to him, and the box of shells, and a little distance away, a bulging plastic sack, wet with the rain and probably full of dead little creatures stuffed in with the torn-up rabbit.

"I'll get someone to get you out after I run over to Mr. Janka's trailer with the money Bernice is bringing to free the fox. She went down to the music store to sell the flute."

"What — are you crazy?" Crow said. "That flute's a hundred years old, for pity's sake! You're not gonna get anything for that piece of junk! My sister got it secondhand in a junk shop a million years ago! D'you think I would have let you have it if I thought I could get any money for it?"

When Crow said that I felt absolutely steaming like hot coals, I was so mad. I guess I'd hung every last hope on that flute. All along, I'd felt so sure it was something of value, something so

fine it was worth all the trouble it had gotten me
into and worth all the mess it would cause with
Dad. I guess I'd thought the flute was priceless.

I guess I'd thought it was charmed.

"It's *got* to be silver," I said more to myself
than to Crow, who was trying to tug off the trap
and couldn't understand how I felt anyway.

"Here comes Bernice — ask her yourself how
much she got for it," Crow said, with his usual
Crow-like sneer.

Bernice was so out of breath she couldn't
speak at all. She just stood there, wiping the
rain from under the visor of her plastic-covered
cap, panting.

A flash of lightning blazed through the sky and
lit us all up brighter than a fluorescent bathroom
light.   Thunder   came   next — BRRAAOOOR
— it sounded like the end of the world. Finally
the rain let up a little and everything grew
quiet.

"Was the flute silver, Bernice?" I asked. I was
so scared she'd say no my voice sounded as if I
had pebbles in my throat.

Bernice shook her had no.

"Not silver?"

No.

"You couldn't sell it?"

No.

BUT. Bernice, still catching her breath, wanted to tell me something. She was reaching into her coat, trying to get something out of the deep yellow pocket of her slicker.

The flute. She pulled it out — it was still in its plastic bag — and held it up.

"Not silver — " she said. She was still panting slightly. "It's *platinum!*"

Platinum?

Crow's mouth flew open. "Don't try to kid me," he said.

"Platinum," Bernice said. She was shaking her head up and down. She was not kidding.

"Real platinum?" I asked. I wasn't even surprised. The perfect way that flute sounded, the music I could get out of it, why, it would have to be something precious and valuable and fantastic. Platinum!

"Probably worth thousands," Bernice said. *"Thousands,"* she repeated. "Mr. Perlberg said he'd never seen one like it before."

Crow let out a growl, a real mad, wolf growl. His face was furious and he seemed to have forgotten about the clamp around his ankle, the rain and the chain that had him shackled to a tree stump.

"I want the flute back," he said. "It's really my flute!"

"You are Outrageous!" Bernice said. "OUT-RAGEOUS! You made a deal. For keeps, remember?"

"I didn't know it was platinum, for pity's sake! Nobody told me it was platinum!"

"You never asked!" Bernice said. "Anyhow, a deal is a deal. Max keeps the flute. You keep the gun. Honorable is honorable."

"Wait a minute," Crow said. "That's not fair! How did I know what I was trading away!"

Bernice's face was getting redder and redder. I never saw her get so mad. She was shaking the flute through the air as if she were leading a fast marching band. "You know what you need, Crow? A bit of flute across the seat of your pants!"

"Hold it, Bernice," I said. I don't like to see Bernice get all worked up; it gets me a little worried. It's just not like her.

"Give him the flute back, Bernice," I said.

Bernice turned around to look at me. She froze with the flute in her hand as if someone were going to take her picture and had told her not to move.

"Give him the flute," I repeated.

114

"What?" Bernice's eyes went round as bull's-eyes. *"What?"*

"I want the gun back," I said.

"You want the *gun* back?" Bernice said. "Are you kidding, Max?"

"I'm not kidding," I said; I felt as if I had swallowed one of Crow's 12-gauge shells and it was resting hard in the bottom of my stomach. "I need it," I said. "I need the gun."

18

Bernice stood there staring at me the longest time, squinting at me from under the visor of her hat.

"I thought I understood kids pretty well, but this is incredible! What for, Max?" she said.

I could hardly answer her.

"Whatever for? Why would you suddenly need the gun?"

"I'm going to shoot the fox," I said, and I went over and picked up Grandpa's gun and a box of shells. The gun felt as if it weighed a hundred pounds it was so heavy. I couldn't believe it had always weighed as much as it weighed now.

"Shoot the fox?" Bernice's voice was a tiny whisper. "Not you, Max!"

"I'd better hurry," I said, and I began to run, because the fox was waiting for me and because I couldn't look at Bernice and because I couldn't talk any more.

"You're not gonna leave me here!" Crow called after me but there was no time for Crow now. Bernice could find someone to free him, sooner or later.

I'd finally understood what the fox had been telling me all along with his eyes: there was another way to save him. He wanted me to kill him.

It was too late to spring the trap. The fox, half dead, wanted no more pain. He did not want to wait for the horror of Mr. Janka's club. He wanted to die quickly.

I rushed back there and kneeled next to him. He was trembling under my jacket, but he opened his eyes to greet me.

"It's all right now," I said, and I started to shake too.

I got up; the rain had stopped but it was almost dark. It was a gray-purple twilight and the wetness made everything shine and gleam all

117

over the place. I tried to pretend that this was just a daydream and that I was at home, lying on my bed in my room; but it didn't work. I was here in the meadow, the gun was stiff in my hands and the fox was waiting to be shot.

I took a few steps back and checked the gun. Crow had left the barrel empty. Though I am not good at loading a gun, I stuck a shell in the way Dad had showed me and heard the click that meant it was ready to be fired.

I tried to think of something else as I raised the gun: I tried to think of school or the way Bernice could make the piccolo sound. I tried to think of next summer and what I'd ask for next Christmas, but all the while I was fitting the gun toe, butt and heel against that dent under my shoulder and feeling the wet metal against my fingers. I was remembering what Dad had said about taking aim; I pointed the barrel at the fox's head and pushed my finger through the trigger guard.

"Don't pull the trigger," Dad had said. "*Snap* the trigger."

For a minute I thought that I wouldn't be able to do it. It was harder than anything I'd ever done before. It was terrifying. It was impossible. What if I missed! But I couldn't miss, standing this close. With a shotgun at this range, no one could miss.

The fox turned his head and looked into my face.

Shoot, his eyes said. Shoot, Max.

I stepped in closer. I held my breath.

I snapped the trigger and the shell flew out of the gun with a terrible force. The noise was worse than thunder and the recoil felt as if it might tear my head right off.

The shell hit the fox I don't know where. Everywhere, I guess. His back legs — even the one in the chain — kicked once in the air and then were still.

He was dead.

The bit of smoke that puffed from the barrel was a cloud between us, getting into my eyes and making them tear.

I started to cough and couldn't stop.

I went down on my knees, still coughing. My eyes felt as if they would never stop burning. It was hard to breathe.

"MAX!"

I looked up, past the beam of the flashlight, into my father's face.

"Where've you been all this time, son? Didn't you know I was coming home?" he said, looking worried. "Your mother's frantic! Told you to be home after school and look at the time! Do you realize what *time* it is?"

I couldn't answer. I couldn't answer at all.

"Max, what'd you shoot this fox for? I'm glad you're practicing your marksmanship, but you're not allowed to shoot a trapped animal. It's not good sportsmanship and besides, you just ruined a perfectly good pelt."

He leaned over and picked up my jacket. "And look at this! Shot your perfectly good jacket full of holes! What the devil were you thinking of, son?"

I couldn't talk. It was like someone had me by the neck and was squeezing with both hands.

"Come on," Dad said. "Mom's had dinner waiting over an hour. Pick up the gun and let's go."

I didn't move. I couldn't move.

"Come on, Max. Didn't you hear me? Pick up the gun and let's go home."

I shook my head.

"What's wrong, Max? Are you sick?"

I shook my head.

"What is it?"

"I don't want to pick up the gun," I said.

"What do you mean?" Dad said. His voice

was sharp. "What do you mean you don't want to pick up the gun?"

"I don't want the gun. I don't want it."

"You don't want Grandpa's gun? Why not?"

"I don't want to shoot anything, Dad. I don't like shooting."

"You don't like shooting? But every boy likes shooting!"

"Not me."

There was a terrible and long silence. Then Dad cleared his throat.

"But you just shot a fox. Why did you shoot the fox?"

I started to cough again. I couldn't answer.

I wished the ghost of my grandfather would suddenly appear and carry me off on his shoulders.

Dad's voice got harder. "Max, why did you shoot the fox?"

I wanted to sound tough as rocks, the way I knew that Dad wanted me to be, but all that came out was a voice that was caught in my throat and had no power in it at all. "He was hurt so bad."

I couldn't see Dad's face, but I saw his breath come out in a cloud of gray mist, like the last bit of smoke from a dying campfire.

He waited a long time before saying anything. "I always wanted you to be as rugged as one of these trees," he finally said. "Invincible. With a bark so tough that you could endure anything."

"He was suffering so much, Dad," I said.

"There are some things we can't let ourselves think too much about."

"I can't help it, Dad."

"So you shot him." It wasn't Dad's voice at all.

"His eyes, Dad. If you could have seen his eyes — "

Dad did not answer. Had he heard me?

"I had to kill him!" I cried.

Because it was dead-still everywhere, I could hear Dad's long sigh. "Max, men have been trapping animals for a long, long time."

"I know it, Dad."

Dark as it was, I could see Dad's eyes glinting, catching little bits of light from somewhere. I knew he was waiting for me to see it his way, to be strong and to agree that I'd never be able to stop what men had been doing for as long as anybody, even Grandpa, could remember. "I don't think you're going to be able to change things, Max."

I couldn't answer for a long time and then, suddenly, I knew I really had to.

"I could try," I said.

Dad stood there just looking and looking at me for what seemed like a year. Finally, he reached over and put an arm around my shoulder. "Yes, you could try," he said.

Then, as if he were talking to himself instead of to me, he whispered, "Maybe I don't really want a Scotch pine for a son after all."

I ran my fingers across my eyelids; my eyes were burning. My fingers were wet. Who could tell? Maybe Grandpa's ghost was right here in his suspenders, listening.

The sky was really dark now — no stars or moon or anything -- just a lot of purple quiet. Dad took out his handkerchief and wiped my face. "Maybe you're not like every boy, Max. What you did took compassion. And courage. Maybe that's why I'm so proud of you."

He took off his jacket, put it around my shoulders and turned his head up to look at the sky. "It's late. Your mother will be worried," he said.

Then he picked up the gun and started to lead the way home. I followed him and tried to think of something good like next summer or next Christmas or the way the flute sounds on a clear day in an open meadow.